MIRACLE in the RAIN

MIRACLE *in the* RAIN

by BEN HECHT

19 43

NEW YORK: ALFRED·A·KNOPF

MIRACLE in the RAIN

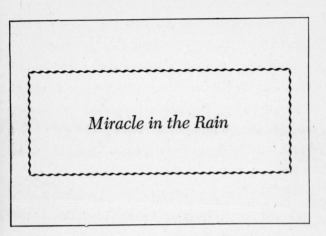

Miracle in the Rain

ANOTHER DAY was ending in New York. A girl walked in the spring rain that bombarded 34th Street. The rain and the twilight hid her. You could see only that she was young, poor and graceful. The girl was carrying a number of bundles. She was on her way home from work to make supper for her mother, who would be sitting at the window in the dark living room looking at the rain. The girl wished her mother would turn on the light and not sit in the dark. But that would never happen. It would always be dark when the girl came into the bare apartment, and her mother would always be sitting in shadows, motionless and staring, as if she were waiting for something. The girl's heart hurt her as she thought of this figure, sitting almost as if it were not alive.

The rain was beginning to leak through her thin coat, and her stockings were wet to the knees. As she moved in the rain she tried not to think of her mother. But there was nothing else of enough importance in her life to think about. She knew the names and faces of a few people in the office. When they talked in the office, they seemed sharply, almost painfully, familiar, but when she left the office at six o'clock these people disappeared. She tried to imagine where they went and what they did and what sort of evenings waited for them behind the doors of their apartments.

The girl in the rain stopped wondering about them because such thoughts made her feel frightened, as if

4

she, too, were disappearing for the night and turning into nobody.

The rain grew stronger and filled the dark with a growing roar. The girl turned into a building for shelter and stood dripping behind glass doors. She was more worried over her bundles than herself. They held cold meats, potato salad, pickles, a loaf of rye bread, a pound of butter and a can of coffee. She had bought these things in the large department store near her office because everything there was a little cheaper than in the stores of her neighborhood.

Now you could see the girl's face in the dim vestibule light. It was a face that might have been pretty if it had not looked so empty and patient. There was no light in its brown eyes and no expression to its full mouth. It was young without youth—an unused face.

A tall young man stopped on his way out of the building and stood beside the girl. He was a soldier and wore a raincoat. After a minute, the young soldier spoke in a voice full of good cheer.

"Look at her go," he said, his eyes admiringly on

5

the bubbling pavement. "Like a pack of horses coming down the homestretch. You know, a night like this makes this town look almost human." He laughed and went on talking. "There's nothing so good as a real rain," he said, "unless it's a blizzard. Listen to her." He pointed happily at the night. "Like firecrackers." His voice grew thoughtful. "I'd be out walking in it right now if I had any place to go. Maybe that's the best time to walk in the rain—when you got nowheres to go."

The girl had glanced at him as he was talking. She was unused to noticing men, and her glance gave her no more than the impression of a young, dark-haired soldier who was full of good cheer.

"It's all in the point of view." The rain admirer smiled at the girl. "If you want to, you can figure you're cast away on a jungle island with nothing and nobody around you but rain. Think how surprised you would be if you were cast away on a jungle island in the rain for ten weeks and you suddenly saw a girl standing beside you." And the soldier laughed again.

"I smell potatoes," he said, "and something like pickles." He was looking at her bundles. "That rain won't let up for hours," he went on. "What do you say we just walk out and let her soak? I'll put your bundles under my coat and they won't get wet. Here, gimme."

He reached out his hands and the girl looked at him and frowned. He had smoky gray eyes and a lean jaw, and his nose looked a little crooked. She wondered how he could talk so friendlily to someone he didn't know at all. She continued to frown, but the soldier seemed not to notice this. His face suddenly seemed to her not at all strange. It was full of liking for her. An impulse not of her mind made her hand him the bundles. He tucked them under his raincoat and opened the door. The rain came bouncing at them.

"All right!" the soldier cried. "Out we go! Come on! Lickety-split!"

He took her arm and they ran together.

"Are we going right?" he demanded. She said nothing and they kept on running. "There's a bus coming,"

7

he announced in her ear. "Do you want to catch it?"

"Yes," said the girl, and felt frightened because she had spoken to a stranger.

"Allez oop!" said the soldier, and pulled her forward at a faster clip. "We can just flag it!"

"Well," said the soldier, sharing a pool of water with her on the bus seat, "we're off the jungle island now and afloat on a raft which I have knocked together with some homemade nails. Have you any idea where we're going?"

"I'm going home," said the girl.

"That's what I figured." The soldier nodded. He looked at her disordered hair sticking to her wet face. "You got a ma or pa or something?" he asked vaguely.

"My mother is home," said the girl in a voice the soldier could barely hear.

"That's wonderful," he said. "Let's get down to brass tacks. My name is Art Hugenon. I'm from Tennessee, only I don't speak it. I've been in town for two days, and have to an extent exhausted most of its points of interest, including all the famous street corners, the top of the Empire State Building and the Zoo. What's your name?" he asked suddenly.

"Ruth Wood," the girl said.

"Ruthie, I can see by looking at you," Private Hugenon continued, "that you are a girl a man can trust. You know, a fella has to be pretty careful in a town like this—particularly a soldier."

Ruth knew he was laughing at her, but when she turned angrily to look at him, she saw a pair of serious eyes regarding her, eyes so full of good will and understanding that she smiled.

"I tell you what," Private Hugenon proceeded. "I'm inviting you and your ma to have dinner with me. Those pickles will keep till tomorrow."

"My mother doesn't go out," said Ruth.

"And you have to go home to her every night for dinner," Private Hugenon said.

"Yes," said Ruth.

"Well, then," the soldier said, "there's nothing left to do but dine at your house."

"You mean you?" said Ruth.

9

"Look at that rain now," said Private Hugenon, pointing out of the bus window. "It's turning somersaults. Woosh-bang!" And he began to laugh as if the rain had suddenly tickled his funny bone.

The girl lay in her narrow bed near the window, unable to sleep. The rain had stopped. A spring moon made a blue flicker in the deep night. The alarm clock said it was almost three, and she must get up at seven, but she wanted to think some more and to remember things. She began the story again for herself at the point where she was opening the apartment door with Mr. Hugenon beside her, skipping the time in the grocery when he bought the chicken and the bottles of beer, because she had been very nervous then. She had worried about his seeing her mother for the first time. But when she had opened the door, he had said, "Good evening, Mrs. Wood." And when her mother didn't answer or even look around, he paid no attention to that. He acted as if it were natural.

"You fix everything up," he said. "I'm going to take

a shower and get shaved. When you see me again I will be looking very pretty."

Ruth smiled at her pillow and skipped again to the supper. It was hard to remember his talk. It was about people he knew. Why should he be so interested in telling her all those things about strangers? And about his aunt too? That was the funniest person she had ever heard of. His aunt must have been really crazy, making him wear long curls and a derby hat when he was only four years old. Ruth frowned into the moonlit room. She should have said something about his mother and father, when he said he didn't have any. But he kept talking and laughing so much you couldn't very well say that.

The girl fidgeted in the narrow bed. She had wanted, all through the evening, to tell him about her mother, so he wouldn't misunderstand her silence and her faraway look, and feel insulted. She explained it all to him now in the moonlit room as she lay remembering. *My mother is very ill, Mr. Hugenon. When I was a little girl, my father left her. And my mother*

11

grew sick. She hasn't spoken for almost ten years. She just sits and stares and cries sometimes, and I take care of her. There's nothing can be done except for me to be with her. She gets frightened when she's alone at night.

He had not even asked how they happened to have such an expensive piano in the apartment when everything else was so different.

We've moved so many times, she explained to a remembered Mr. Hugenon, *and each time we've taken the piano with us, although nobody has ever played it. It belonged to my father. He used to play it all the time, and I can remember that when I was a little girl I used to sit in my mother's lap and we would listen to him composing music and playing it over and over.*

She remembered Mr. Hugenon going to the piano and how her mother had stared at him as he sat down.

It must be terribly late, the girl thought, looking out of the window at the deep night, but she wanted to see Mr. Hugenon at the piano again, banging away

12

despite it was so out of tune, and singing much better than most of the singers you hear on the radio. She remembered herself sitting stiffly in the chair and not saying anything or trying to join in the singing. She wished desperately now that she had smiled or laughed and talked back to him, instead of sitting like a stick. But she had felt so excited, so happy, that he must have known it. She smiled now at the dark, remembering him again at the piano, playing and singing and loving them—her and her mother.

Loving her and her mother—the words made her blush. "But he did," the girl said softly to herself, and that was why everything had been so wonderful. It was as if she and her poor mother who never smiled were part of something that belonged to Mr. Hugenon, and he wanted them to be as happy as he was.

What a remarkable thing to have happen, she dreamed; that there should be so much fun in her house, that a tall young soldier should stand laughing on its worn carpet and recite poetry while he drank beer. He was a crazy one. The girl's mind grew dim.

A smile covered her face as if a light were shining on it. And under this light she fell asleep.

Ruth stood on the corner of 45th Street and watched the people swarm by till her eyes ached. It was Saturday afternoon and the April day glowed as if it had come to Broadway from a meadow. Beside Ruth stood a middle-aged woman who, despite the sun, looked a little frost-bitten. This was because the tip of her nose was red and her eyes watery and squinting. She was Miss Ullman, and was Ruth's immediate superior in the office, having full charge of the Atlantic Novelty Company's ledgers. A skimpy fur was around her shoulders and a sort of three-decker hat sat on her gray hair. A lopsided coat hung from her shoulders. "I don't see what you want me along for," said Miss Ullman. "He certainly didn't ask to have me along."

"I don't happen to know him," said Ruth. "I mean I've never been out with him."

"Or anybody else," said Miss Ullman, with a sniff.

"It's really unbelievable, such idiocy. I could have been home fixing up things." Miss Ullman lived in a room that looked out on a brick wall. She had sat in it so long that she felt remiss when she was away from it. She looked slyly at the flushed face of her assistant. "No use breaking your neck rubbering," she said. "He won't be along for some time. We're early."

A great change came over the swarm of people moving toward the waiting girl. They became friendly people, full of meaning, for walking among them was Private Hugenon. His coat was unbuttoned and he was making faces, cocking his head from side to side, so that you almost had to laugh, looking at him. Then Ruth saw that he wasn't making faces, but whistling. As he came nearer a fear smote her that he would be angry at the presence of Miss Ullman, and she wished with all her heart that she had not been such a fool as to invite her.

"Ahoy," said Private Hugenon. "I got lost. That's why I'm not here ahead of time."

"I want you to meet Miss Ullman," Ruth said. . . .

15

"This is Mr. Hugenon, Miss Ullman."

"How do you do," Miss Ullman said in a squeaky voice. "Well, I guess I'd better run along now."

"Nothing doing." Mr. Hugenon took her arm. "I've reserved a table for three."

"But you didn't know," Ruth said. But Mr. Hugenon looked at her owlishly down his slightly crooked nose and winked.

"I know everything," he said, and swept on with his guests.

Ruth saw Miss Ullman looking sideways at him as they walked through the crowd, and she began to worry that Mr. Hugenon would not be so clever as he had been in her home. She wished Miss Ullman had heard him the night before.

But Ruth's worries were unwarranted. At the table in the restaurant Mr. Hugenon was even more remarkable than he had been the night before. Miss Ullman laughed at almost everything he said. Her squinty little eyes became invisible and her gray head kept bobbing with mirth. Ruth laughed, too, and when she

16

did, Mr. Hugenon beamed and leaned toward her as if he were going to put his arm around her. But he didn't touch her at all. Instead, he embraced Miss Ullman and said, "I have three tickets to the theater and I insist on your coming."

"For heaven's sake," said Miss Ullman, "that's really not necessary. No, you children run along and have fun."

"Nothing doing," said Mr. Hugenon. "If you leave, a blight will descend on me. I will get the hiccups and bump into my sergeant."

Ruth thought he couldn't have three tickets, but it pleased her that he should lie about it. They had some difficulty finding the particular theater Mr. Hugenon had in mind, but finally they all ended up safely in the third row. Here the afternoon disappeared in a haze of music and bright lights shining on dancers, acrobats and comedians. Miss Ullman sat spellbound and Ruth stared at the stage with her mouth opened in a continuous smile of delight.

It was twilight when they came into the street. The

day had grown chill and unfriendly. Everything seemed noisy and scattered, and the faces crowding by seemed part of some sudden disillusion.

"I've got to go home and get supper," said Ruth.

"Of course," said Mr. Hugenon, and kept staring into the street. "This town certainly gives you the willies. Look, it's full of blind people. It's a wonder they don't bump into each other or all get run over." He turned to Ruth and smiled. "We're all going home with you and pick up some things on the way, so stop worrying. . . . How do you feel about some caviar tonight, Miss Ullman?"

"Oh, for heaven's sakes," the little bookkeeper squeaked, and hung onto her three-decker hat. "Oh, my, I've never had any. I'm sure it's awful."

"A very sensible attitude," said Mr. Hugenon, and they joined the blind people in the street. They came to an open store in which a crowd was standing. An auctioneer was intoning information at them.

"Wait a minute." Mr. Hugenon stopped in the doorway. "What's going on here?"

"It's one of those auctions," said the worldly Miss Ullman. "I wouldn't go near them."

They stood listening to the auctioneer, and Mr. Hugenon edged his guests inside. The auctioneer was talking through his nose.

"We have next this genuine Roman coin," he was saying into a small microphone, "a priceless antique dug up from the tomb of the Caesars. Examine it, please. A genuine Roman coin, such as would make any collector's mouth water. Think of what this piece of gold has seen! If it could only talk, it would tell you the story of the Roman emperors—all of them! I am offering you this museum piece at your own price. What am I bid for this bit of fabled metal?"

"Oh, I want to buy it," Ruth whispered suddenly. She looked, shining-eyed, at Mr. Hugenon and raised her voice. "Two dollars!" she called out.

"Two dollars!" repeated the auctioneer angrily. "I am bid two dollars for this priceless antique! Think of it! Do I hear three? Three? Do I hear three?"

He heard nothing of the sort, and then, fearful the

19

bird in the hand might fly through the door, he announced, "Sold! Sold for two dollars! Or should I say given away? . . . This way, lady!"

Mr. Hugenon examined the genuine Roman coin as they rode toward 85th Street in the bus.

"It looks quite antique," said Miss Ullman, her head bent over. "That says 'the Era of Vespasian.' He was a Roman emperor, all right. I wonder if that hole belongs in it or if somebody made it recently. You can't tell about Roman coins." She looked up at Ruth and added, "Whatever made you buy it?"

"I don't really know," said Ruth. "I just had to have it. . . . It's for you," she added shyly, looking at Mr. Hugenon.

"I'm going to wear it around my neck for a lucky piece," he smiled at her, and added in a dramatic voice:

> *"Around his neck he wore*
> *The Maid Utrilda's charm,*
> *The little silver crucifix*
> *That keeps a man from harm."*

20

Miss Ullman nodded in wonder. And Ruth tried to keep the tears from showing in her eyes. She thought she would never sleep again, but lie awake night after night remembering everything.

The office people were much impressed by the transformation of Miss Ullman's assistant. She sat at her desk and glowed, and her voice saying "Good morning" was so full of happiness that two of the filing clerks felt themselves definitely smitten. Even Mr. Jalonick, the red-faced manager, gave her a curious look as he passed her desk on Tuesday and said, "How are you?"

Ruth beamed at him and her heart, which was full, overflowed in a smile. But she spoke neither to the all-powerful Mr. Jalonick nor to the two ogling clerks, nor to anyone. She found it even difficult to speak to herself, for so much had happened that you didn't know where to begin remembering it. There had been parties in her home and the piano had sounded every night. There had also been singing,

21

and Miss Ullman had given imitations of the people in the office that were wonderful. And last night Art had turned on the radio and danced with her in the kitchen and recited poetry:

> *"Ariadne arose*
> *From her couch in the snows——"*

But there were more important things. For instance, Art sending her mother flowers, and how her mother had sat staring at them all evening and finally smiled. She had seen the smile, although it was almost too faint to notice, and her heart had almost burst with happiness.

The days passed swiftly and this was already Friday noon. All the days and nights were so joined together in a single glow of excitement that Saturday afternoon and all day Sunday were almost here again. She realized this with a catch at her heart as if someone had knocked the breath out of her. When she stood up to go to lunch, her legs were unsteady.

She came out of the dark building and felt bewildered by the sun for a moment. Above the neighborhood smells of coffee, gasoline and old buildings, a fresh, exciting odor lay in the air, as if the sky were a garden. Ruth took a deep breath and started to walk, when she heard someone running behind her. She turned and saw Art. He took her arm.

"I'm glad I caught you," he said. "Do you mind just standing here and talking, because I've only got about ten minutes? I'm leaving, you see. They just told me a half hour ago and I'm supposed to be on my way to the boat. I can say I got lost for a few minutes."

"You're leaving?" said Ruth. "For where?"

"Overseas," said Art. "I've only got time to say goodby. And listen, write me, will you? Send your letters to this address." He put a slip of paper in her hand. "They'll be forwarded. And don't worry if you don't hear from me for some time. I'll be off the mailman's route for quite a while."

23

"Oh, Art," said Ruth, and leaned against the building.

"Darling," said Art. He looked at her for a moment, his smoky gray eyes smiling, his wide mouth turned up eagerly. Then he put his arms around her and held her tightly. "Write me, please," he whispered. "I'll think of you every minute."

"Yes," said Ruth.

"I'm wearing the lucky piece you gave me," said Art, "the genuine Roman coin. So you don't have to worry about anything. And I don't either." He looked at her now as if he were going to cry out something wild, and a number of people who were going to lunch in 29th Street turned curiously toward the spectacle of a tall soldier holding a girl in his arms.

"I love you, Ruth," he whispered. "You don't know how wonderful you are. Nobody does. Only me. Darling, kiss me once, so I can remember on the jungle island."

Her lips felt his face, then his mouth. She was conscious of his face gleaming close to her, of his warm lips, and for the minute they stood together she felt as if the sky had come down and covered her with all its beauty.

"Good-by," the whisper said on her lips. When she opened her eyes she was alone.

After the supper dishes were washed and put away, Ruth sat each night writing. It took two or three nights to finish a letter. Finding the words that would say the things she felt, required time. But she loved this time. She dreamed of it all day. During the day when pain rose in her throat she had only to remember that in a few hours she would be writing his name and speaking to him.

Her mother sat watching her as she wrote, but she didn't mind this. Sometimes she even wrote about her mother: "Oh, Art, I understand her so much better now. Because she is waiting for someone who will never come back, and that is so much worse than waiting for someone who will very soon come back. And it is no wonder she has never smiled or spoken to anyone, because how could you if someone you were waiting for never came back? Oh, Art, when I see you again I will look at you so long you will think I am crazy."

Miss Ullman sat in the crowded lunchroom with her assistant and talked about Private Hugenon.

"It's too bad we didn't ask him some questions," she said. "Then we would know where his folks live and might get some news about him from them."

"I don't think he has any folks," said Ruth. "Besides, I'll get a letter just as soon as anybody, I'm sure."

"It's two months," said Miss Ullman.

"But he's way on the other side of the world," said Ruth, and turned her eyes to the newspaper beside her plate of scrambled eggs.

"Did he ever say what branch of the service he was in?" Miss Ullman insisted.

"No," said Ruth, "he didn't, because I didn't ask him." Her eyes grew tearful and she added softly, "I never asked him about anything. I just didn't think to ask him."

Miss Ullman ate in silence and watched the flushed face of her assistant bent over the newspaper. She noticed Ruth was reading a story of American troops fighting in the Solomon Islands.

It was a hot night. Ruth sat at the table in the living room, writing. The three months of writing letters were a timeless memory in her heart. The things that happened, the streets growing light and turning dark —these did not make days for her. She looked at the room in shadow and at the piano. She could hear again his voice and watch his smile and the way he moved. And as always when she brought him to her eyes, a panic turned her heart over, and she could not think for a moment, but only feel as she had felt that only time when he had kissed her.

But all remembered things that had actually been were a small part of her treasure. The greater part was something outside the reach of words. It would be there in the morning streets, in the faces of the crowd, in the tall buildings, in the sky and the window signs and the office people. It was the glow of friendliness that surrounded her wherever she moved. She had become part of everything she saw, as if the world were eager to embrace her. Her heart, so long used to sitting like a lonely child in the dark, found company everywhere now. Everything that smiled or moved or stood still and looked beautiful was its companion. And all the joy that life gave her now she brought like a gift to the image of her faraway soldier.

The doorbell rang and Ruth looked up from her letter. The ringing of the doorbell frightened her, so she could not move for a moment. No doorbells ever rang in her home at this hour. The mailman handed her the letter and asked her to sign her name in the book. The heat-heavy night pressed against her as if it were another visitor on the steps.

She closed the door and opened the letter. It was not from him. It was typewritten and very neat. It was

engraved on top. Her heart was pounding too much
and she couldn't read it. But the typewritten words
were already in her head. They said Arthur Hugenon
was dead. They notified her he had died bravely in
battle in an advance against the enemy. She was be-
ing notified because Private Hugenon had requested
that if anything happened to him, word be sent to her
alone. Then she read the letter again. But although
the words jumped about, they failed to change. Private Hugenon was dead. He had been killed in an
advance on the enemy in the jungle surrounding
Guadalcanal.

Oh, yes, the jungle, thought Ruth. He had always
talked about the jungle. She stopped to remember,
and the words went clearly through her head, "Think
how surprised you would be if you were cast away
on a jungle island in the rain for ten weeks and you
suddenly saw a girl standing beside you."

Private Hugenon was so alive as he said this over
in her head that the letter seemed to tell a horrible
lie. She read it again. Then she stood still and looked

at nothing. Her mind felt white, as if everything had disappeared from it. Private Hugenon stood beside the piano, his head lowered, his wide mouth tipped in a smile, his humorous nose and humorous eyes a bit pensive, and said to her he was dead somewhere in a jungle. But she did not answer him. She turned her back on the piano and went to her bed. She undressed slowly and lay down. She stared at the ceiling and tried to think of something. But no thoughts would come to her. When the alarm clock rang at a quarter to seven, her eyes were still open and her heart still empty, as if the heat-heavy night had blotted it out.

The office people buzzed with the tragedy of the bookkeeper's assistant. They looked furtively at the pale girl and felt themselves near to heroism. A soldier one of them had loved had died bravely in battle, and this brought the war into the office and stood it beside every desk.

Miss Ullman went to lunch with her assistant each

day and went home with her after work. She was worried about the silent, placid face of her friend.

When they were alone she said, "Come on, let's talk about him. It'll be better if you do. Remember, I was his friend too."

To this Ruth answered, "There's nothing to talk about."

"You might tell me what you're thinking," Miss Ullman said.

"I'm not thinking about anything," Ruth said.

This was true during the daytime. During the night Ruth lay and looked for hours into the humorous face of Private Hugenon. He stood in the corner, his head slightly lowered, and regarded her pensively. Or sometimes he raised his head and his mouth smiled as if he were going to laugh. When she saw him thus in her mind, a hand seized her heart as if it were going to squeeze it into nothing.

The change that came to Ruth began to worry Miss Ullman. She could not understand how anyone as sweet as Ruth could become so bitter and hard. It would have been easy to understand if she had cried and been unable to come to work because of grief. But Ruth came to work every day on time and never cried, but grew more and more rasping, and took to sneering at everybody. And in her home she spoke angrily to her mother and ordered her to bed. Miss Ullman, wondering how to help her friend, could think of nothing except to remain at her side as much as was possible.

One Sunday, walking in the park, Ruth turned to her and said suddenly, in a voice that made her shiver, "I hate this. I hate them all." She was looking at the people lying on the sunny grass. "You always keep asking me what I think. Well, I'll tell you. I want to die, because I hate everything. I can't stand it."

Ruth began to shake and Miss Ullman's arm went around her.

"Sit down, dear," she said.

"I don't want to sit down," said Ruth, and raised her voice. "It's such a damn fake. The music playing and people walking around. So damn smug. You too. Everybody. I don't want to see you any more."

Ruth pulled herself away from her friend's arm and ran off through the park. Miss Ullman could not understand Ruth because she herself had never known hope.

On Monday morning Miss Ullman waited eagerly for her assistant. She looked quickly at her face when she came in. It was cold and without the light of greeting.

At six o'clock Miss Ullman said, "Do you mind if I go home with you?"

"I'm not going home," said Ruth. "What should I go home for? If she's too sick to get her supper, let her go without any."

The two went to a small restaurant and sat in a dim corner. Neither spoke. Here, for the first time, Ruth cried. Her tears began unexpectedly. She stood up blindly and walked out of the restaurant. Miss Ullman went with her.

They walked together until Ruth came to the corner where they had once stood waiting on a Saturday afternoon for the appearance of Private Hugenon.

Here the girl stopped and half hid herself in a dark doorway and stood looking with streaming eyes into the crowded street.

The little bookkeeper finally took Ruth's arm and said in a shaking voice, "Oh, please, let's go somewhere."

Ruth followed her without asking where, and an idea came to Miss Ullman. As they walked through the war-dimmed streets the girl's head drooped and she moved without sight, guided by Miss Ullman's hand on her arm. Behind her tears a thought repeated itself dully. She wanted to die. Everything that had been so wonderful—the faces of people and the tall buildings, the sky and the window lights—these were gone. She was back again in the little corner where she had always sat like a lonely child. But the corner was darker now and the loneliness deeper, and she would rather die than return to it. Her dream was gone, and her hope, and the magic smile lay dead in

34

a jungle. Thus she moved, guided by the little book-keeper, up a flight of wide stone steps.

"I thought we would go in here," said Miss Ullman. "It's St. Patrick's Cathedral. It's very nice inside. And very restful. You don't have to do anything. Just sit down and rest." And she walked through the outer doors into the body of the cathedral, holding the girl's arm.

The hush and height of the great room startled the weeping girl. Dark wings seemed to spread above her. Around her a light glowed faintly, as if fearful of breaking a silence. And far away, as if this were not a room but a wide land with beacons, candles shone.

The girl stood awed by a sense of invisible elegance, and her eyes looked frightenedly for Miss Ullman. She saw the little bookkeeper kneeling in an empty space with her head hung, as if there were nothing to see in all this sweep of shadows and shrines.

Ruth remained standing against the wall. The tears dried in her eyes and she could see more plainly the many-pointed golden altar in the distance and the statues along the wall before which red and yellow candle cups were burning. Then she saw how almost empty the rows on rows of benches were. In the great and vaulted room sat only a handful of people—a sailor and an old man, a trembling old woman and a young man and woman together, making a lonely pattern of attendance. The figures she could see did not seem to be praying, but merely sitting, as if they were resting from something. *They're all thinking of God,* Ruth said to herself, and the words confused her as if she had said something silly.

No usher appeared, but finally the very silence came to her elbow and bade her move. She started walking down the aisle in front of the statues. *Oh,* she thought, *they're supposed to be saints.*

The saints stood in niches behind a marble rail with candles in front of them, and they looked festive and well attended, even though all the worshiping places were empty. The girl walked by the beckoning marble effigies heedlessly, a lonely figure in a lonely place. None of the tender and graceful statues tempted her to pause, and as she moved by them the darkness in her heart seemed to grow. The people of heaven, like the people of the streets, were strangers, and all the grandeur and history of the great hollow room beat down in vain on her small, forlorn figure.

She paused finally because the candle-lighted aisle had grown dark. There was another statue behind the marble rail, but she could barely see it. No candles were lit in front of it. It stood in the dark, unfestive and unattended.

Staring at this white figure in the shadows, Ruth felt her body grow warm with tears. Why should there be one even in heaven who was lonely and stood in the dark? Why did everybody light candles for the others and none for him? Her hands clung to the marble rail and she shivered as her eyes peered into the shadows. The other statues had been strangers, even though they bore the names of God's friends, but this one she knew. She knew what it was to stand in the dark unnoticed. Trembling, she knelt to read the plate on the marble rail. It said that this unattended one was Saint Andrew, famed for his generosity and self-effacement, and that he had been the first friend of Jesus.

When she stood up, Miss Ullman was beside her. Ruth turned a flushed face to her.

"Why hasn't he got any candles?" she whispered. "You'd think somebody would pay attention to him."

Her eyes turned wildly to the many cups glowing before the image of Saint Theresa. She hesitated and then moved quickly to the saint's shrine. She took two of the yellow lights and put one on each side of Saint Andrew. The candle cups filled the holy niche with a glow, and for a moment the brightness startled the girl as if it came from somewhere else. The statue looked down on her with the sudden intimacy of light in its long, bearded face—looked down on her and into her heart that glowed back brightly, as if the two candles were burning there.

Ruth's conversion was a matter shared only by Saint Andrew and Miss Ullman. Every evening after work Ruth stopped on her way home to put two fresh candles in the place, one on each side of the statue.

Miss Ullman often went with her and knelt to pray in silence. Her friend neither knelt nor prayed, but stood for several minutes looking up at the lean, tender face of the saint and then went on home to make the supper.

One evening when she was alone, Ruth stood before the lighted saint and felt a long misery end in her heart—the misery of loneliness and of vanished hope. The friendless streets that led nowhere, the smiling face of her soldier that returned again and again to send its look through her, like a knife falling on her heart—these and all the dark, silent hours in which she lived went suddenly away from her, like a bad dream ending.

She knelt before the glowing statue and began to whisper. She informed Saint Andrew of the way she had met Mr. Hugenon and of all the things he had said to her. When she walked out of the church her face was smiling.

Thereafter the girl talked each evening to the saint.

She knew no prayers and had no religious habits from childhood to guide her conferences with the lean, bearded face, aglow in the holy niche. But all through her day in the office her heart was filled with the knowledge that a friend waited for her in the great hollow room of the church. She could tell him of all the secret things she had dreamed after the soldier went away, and of the apartment she had planned to furnish when he came back to marry her. She could tell him of the letters she had written which he had never received, and of the sort of life they would have lived—a very wonderful life that would have kept on and on, growing more full of love and happiness each year. And at the end of these conferences, Ruth grew silent and looked up intently at the lean, bearded face above her. Then she whispered eagerly, "Oh, please take care of him."

Miss Ullman considered that a miracle had happened, because she was certain that Saint Andrew had saved her friend from death. A miracle thus entering the little bookkeeper's life, which heretofore had been barren even of events, overwhelmed all her days. As the one who had led the grieving girl to the cathedral, Miss Ullman felt a proprietary interest in the miracle. Her dried little face shone with the great secret and her heart was filled with joy. Although the miracle had not been for her, she was so thrilled by her nearness to the wonder that even the musty office in which she had toiled so monotonously for twenty years became a place of enchantment. And there were great riches in the musty room that looked out on the brick wall, for here she sat frantically hugging the knowledge of grace that had come from heaven.

In the office Miss Ullman managed to remain a little bookkeeper with a steady eye for the profundities of her ledgers. But after hours she flew from bookstore to bookstore, inquiring for books about the first friend of Christ. "We ought to know something about him," she explained to Ruth, "because he's doing so much."

But they could find out nothing. Apparently, no books had ever been written about this man, famed so long ago for his self-effacement. There were many books about other saints, whole shelves of them, but store after store reported that no information existed about Saint Andrew. This pleased Ruth. She preferred her saint unattended and uncelebrated, as he had been the evening she had found him standing in the shadows. That was why she could talk to him, because he knew, without her explaining anything, how it felt to be hidden in a dark corner.

In her room one evening, Miss Ullman spoke to her friend about taking their long-deferred vacation together. All through the summer Ruth had refused to leave Saint Andrew.

"I couldn't go away," Ruth said. "I really can't."

"You mean about the candles," said Miss Ullman. Ruth nodded.

"We could arrange to have someone else put them there," Miss Ullman said.

"You go first"—Ruth shook her head—"and when

42

you come back maybe I'll go somewhere. But I don't want to, really. I want to stay here."

She looked out of the window at the brick wall with so rapt a smile that Miss Ullman knew this was best.

When the little bookkeeper boarded the train for the country a few weeks later, she was worried about her friend, who had caught cold. It was a chilly October day and Ruth was sneezing a great deal.

"Take care of yourself," Miss Ullman cautioned, "because you mustn't get sick while I'm away."

"I won't, don't worry," said Ruth, and then, in a low voice, added, "Write me; don't forget."

The train started and Ruth watched it with a dizzy head. Her temples throbbed and her hands felt hot. She came into the street where a gloomy afternoon hung like a cold cloud. It was Saturday and her work was done. She took a bus to the cathedral.

Inside she procured fresh candles and placed them in front of her saint. She knelt, whispering for a long time, and the glowing statue swam before her. Her body felt watery, her mouth was dry and her words became mixed up. But despite all these things, she felt happy and continued relating to Saint Andrew the manner in which her soldier had said good-by to her. "He was very unhappy," she whispered, "just as I was. And I don't know how long he held me in his arms. But it was a very long time, and then he said, 'Write me letters, lots of letters,' and he said he loved me."

It was night when she was done telling of these matters to Saint Andrew and whispering her last words, "Oh, please take care of him." She felt so warm and dizzy that she was almost unable to walk down the steps outside the cathedral.

After supper she went to bed and her mother sat beside her. She fell asleep with her mother's hand on her forehead. On Sunday, Ruth stayed in bed till the afternoon. Her mother watched her with sad, far-away eyes when she got up and dressed.

"I'll be back soon," she said, and hurried off to the cathedral. Here there were many people at worship, and the organ was playing. Ruth was aware of none

of these things. She stood in the back of the great
hollow room for a time until her legs grew strong
enough to walk. Then she made her way unsteadily
down the aisle to Saint Andrew. She put new candles
in place and knelt before the shrine. But she was too
dizzy to whisper. After many minutes she looked up
at the glowing face of her friend and said, "Darling,
please write me a letter."

Then she fell forward. One of the priests who had
often seen her kneeling at the shrine came to her and
lifted her up. Her purse yielded her name and address and a doctor was called. She was taken home
and put to bed. The doctor said she had pneumonia
of an active sort and must remain in bed for several
weeks.

Ruth lay for five days, attended at intervals by the
doctor. On the night of the fifth day she opened her
eyes and looked weakly around her. Her mother was
sitting in the dark, staring out of the bedroom window. Ruth heard a sound that confused her. She listened a long time and recognized the rain falling.

Too weak to move, she lay with her eyes open and gleaming, and listened to the wild hammer of the rain in the dark.

Suddenly there came to her an anxiety. There was something wrong, something she could not find in her dim mind. She tried to think what it was. After a long time it came to her. She saw the dark niche and the statue, unfestive and unattended. There were no candles around her saint. He was standing in the shadows.

The sick girl pushed herself upright in her bed. Her body felt made of paper, but she found strength with which to dress. She dressed slowly, careful not to tumble over. Her mother watched her in silence and Ruth smiled. This time she was pleased that her mother never spoke, for she would have said something wrong. She would have said, "Don't go out, Ruth. You're very sick and it's raining hard. You can't walk. You have fever. You mustn't go."

The words grew faint in the girl's mind and she stood fully dressed. The pains and discomforts had all left her. There remained only a lightness, as if wings were moving her out of the dark apartment into the rain-bounding street.

The night exploded around her. Cold wind and sharp rain roared in the dark. Heedless of the storm, the sick girl moved through the splashing street and saw only a shadowed figure waiting for her candles. She continued onward, down streets filled with storm, and she no longer knew where she was going. She could see the place in her mind—the hushed, high room, the shadows beating like wings under the vaulted ceiling, the shrines glowing with red and yellow cups. It seemed so close and so real that she smiled into the downpour and continued moving through it, dreaming that each step must bring her into the vision before her.

The dream grew brighter and she no longer knew if she were still moving in the rain or already standing in the cathedral. She paused, bewildered by a burst of thunder, and the storm beat her against a dark wall. Here a voice suddenly spoke to her. She turned and looked into the wild night.

"Ruthie," said the voice. "Good heavens, I'm glad I caught you. Come in here and let me look at you. Oh, Ruthie, let me look at your face."

It was Private Hugenon, grinning from ear to ear.

"Art!" she said. "Oh, Art, is it really you?"

"It isn't the King of England," said the soldier, and stood beaming at her until she thought she must faint for joy.

"You've come back," she whispered.

"Of course I've come back," Private Hugenon laughed. "What did you think—I'd stay away? Ruthie, I'm so glad to see you I'm going to start yelling like an Indian."

"You didn't write me," Ruth whispered.

"You can't send letters when there are no mailmen," said Private Hugenon. "What this war needs is more mailmen at the front."

"Oh, Art," Ruth gasped, "you've come back!" Her eyes stayed on him hungrily. "You're just the same," she whispered. "Tell me, is everything else still the same as it was?"

"Infinitely worse," Private Hugenon's smoky eyes smiled on her. "I love you so much I can't sleep or eat or anything. It was like living cast away in a jungle, without you. Come here; I want to hold you. Remember, it was raining like this when I saw you the first time? Remember?"

"Oh, yes," said Ruth. *9 407 4*

"I got all your letters," said Private Hugenon, with his arms around her. "And look." He removed an object that hung from his neck. "Remember this?"

"It's the lucky piece I gave you," said Ruth.

"The genuine Roman coin," Private Hugenon said softly. "Here, you keep it now. I don't need it any more."

"You're not going back?" Ruth's hands clung to him.

"No, nevermore," said the soldier. "I'm here to stay. Like this—with you in my arms forever and ever."

She raised her face, glowing as if many candles were burning about her head, and Private Hugenon pressed his lips against hers.

Two days later Miss Ullman came back to her office. She had been worried over not hearing from Ruth. She looked nervously at the girl's empty desk and went directly into Mr. Jalonick's office.

Mr. Jalonick looked very serious. He told her that the police had called him an hour ago and notified him that Ruth Wood was dead. A priest had identified her. She had been lying in the morgue unclaimed since Wednesday.

Miss Ullman stared a long time at her employer and then said slowly, "It can't be." She was thinking of Saint Andrew.

The heart of the little bookkeeper was heavy and dark as she entered the long, boxlike building of the morgue. She wandered through the half-lit corridors of this terminus until she came to a door marked BUREAU OF MISSING PERSONS.

The police lieutenant nodded at the small gray-haired woman weeping beside his desk.

"Yes," he said kindlily, "we found her in the street the morning after the big storm. I guess she must have been out of her head, because she had pneumonia and evidently got up out of bed while delirious and tried to go somewhere."

"Yes, I know," said Miss Ullman. "Could I see her just once, please?"

"Sure," said the police lieutenant.

Miss Ullman was led into the room of the dead. The lieutenant pulled back the sheet on one of the slabs. Ruth's face, thin and white, looked up at them. The wasted cheeks and the fever-thinned mouth were fixed as if in a childlike sleep.

"She has something in her hand," said Miss Ullman, after a long pause. "Look, she's holding something."

"That's right," said the lieutenant. "I hadn't noticed."

He uncurled the clenched fingers and removed a small object.

"What is it? Do you know?" He held it up.

Miss Ullman stood staring at the thing in his hand. She was unable to speak, because something like fright pounded in her heart. Staring and with her mouth opened, Miss Ullman managed to take a step nearer.

"Oh, my!" she moaned. "Oh, look at it! Oh, my!"

She was looking at a coin—an old Roman coin with a hole in its top. Printed on its edge was the phrase "Era of Vespasian."

"Do you know what it is?" the lieutenant repeated.

"Yes," said the little bookkeeper in a whisper. "It's a genuine Roman coin. It belonged to somebody who——"

But Miss Ullman did not finish her statement. Her face grew radiant. She smiled wildly at the coin and at the gentle face of her dead friend. Then she fell to her knees and began praying, and her squeaky little voice, rapt and joyous, filled the room of the dead.

A NOTE ON THE TYPE

The text of this book is set in Caledonia, a Linotype face designed by W. A. Dwiggins, the man responsible for so much that is good in contemporary book design and typography. Caledonia belongs to the family of printing types called "modern face" by printers—a term used to mark the change in style of type-letters that occurred about 1800. It has all the hard-working feet-on-the-ground qualities of the Scotch Modern face plus the liveliness and grace that is integral in every Dwiggins "product" whether it be a simple catalogue cover or an almost human puppet.

The book was composed, printed, and bound by H. Wolff, New York. The typography and design are by George Salter.